STEVE WEATHERILL studied at Hornsey College
of Art and the Royal College of Art. A freelance
cartoonist and illustrator, he created The Rat Race
cartoon strip for the *Financial Times*, and is the author
and illustrator of the successful *Lucy Goose* books.
Steve lives in Lincolnshire with his wife, two young
children and Goz the gosling.

It's a warm sunny day in April.

Knock, knock!

Who's there?

He's just hatched.

But the nest is empty.

Goz is all alone.

Then he sees a long
green leg.

Then he sees two grey pointed ears and a tail.

Then he sees a wagging
brown tail.

Then he sees two big orange feet.

And it's time for your first swim!